Butterfly Meadow

Dazzle's Prickly Problem

Olivia Moss

Illustrated by Sam Chaffey

SCHOLASTIC

With special thanks to Narinder Dhami

First published in the UK in 2008 by Scholastic Children's Books
An imprint of Scholastic Ltd
Euston House, 24 Eversholt Street
London, NW1 1DB, UK
Registered office: Westfield Road, Southam, Warwickshire, CV47 0RA
SCHOLASTIC and associated logos are trademarks and /
or registered trademarks of Scholastic Inc.
Series created by Working Partners Ltd.

Text copyright © Working Partners, 2008
Illustration copyright © Sam Chaffey, 2008

The moral right of the author and illustrator
of this work has been asserted by them.

Cover illustration © Sam Chaffey, 2008

ISBN 978 1 407 10658 8

Printed by
CPI Bookmarque, Croydon, CR0 4TD
Papers used by Scholastic Children's Books are made
from wood grown in sustainable forests.

For Courtney Mitchell ~ a true friend

CONTENTS

CHAPTER ONE

Fun in the Orchard

"Are we all ready?" Dazzle called excitedly, fluttering her pale yellow wings. "Here we go!"

Dazzle and her friends, Skipper, Twinkle and Mallow, were playing in the apple orchard by Butterfly Meadow. They'd found a big fallen leaf balanced on the branch of an apple tree and were using it as a see-saw. Dazzle and Twinkle perched on one side of the leaf, with Skipper and Mallow were on the other. They rocked it to and fro as fast as they could.

Dazzle loved seeing how the bright

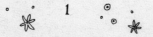

sunshine filtered through the leaves and made the colours of her friends' wings glow. On such a lovely day, Dazzle didn't have a care in the world. All she wanted was to go higher and higher!

"Let's bounce even more, Dazzle!" Twinkle suggested.

The two butterflies flew up into the air and then dove down on to the leaf. The other side of the leaf tipped and sent Mallow and Skipper sailing up towards the sky.

"Yay!" Skipper laughed with delight, as she fluttered her wings. "This is great fun!"

"Now it's our turn," Twinkle said eagerly.

Skipper and Mallow flew up high, just like Dazzle and Twinkle had done, and then swooped down on to their side of the leaf. Dazzle and Twinkle soared into the air.

"Wheee!" the two butterflies cried in delight.

Dazzle felt her tummy turn over. She couldn't wait to have another go! She was so lucky to have good friends like Skipper, Mallow and Twinkle to play with in the orchard.

"It's our turn now," Mallow called. But as Dazzle and Twinkle came to rest on the other side of the leaf, a gruff voice rang through the air.

"Excuse me!"

The four butterflies froze and looked at one another in surprise.

"Who said that?" asked Skipper, looking around the apple tree.

"I did!" the voice replied.

"It's coming from down there," said Dazzle, pointing with her wing to the ground.

The butterflies all peered through the leaves. Standing at the bottom of the tree trunk they saw two spiky hedgehogs snuffling in the grass.

"Have you seen any hedgehogs around the orchard today?" the biggest one called.

"Only you two," Twinkle said, grinning.

The hedgehogs glanced at each other. The smaller hedgehog shook its head slowly.

"What's wrong?" asked Dazzle as she and her friends flew down.

"We can't find our son, Prickle, anywhere,"

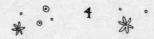

4

the father hedgehog said, peering among the clumps of grass at the bottom of the tree. "We were hoping you might have seen him."

"Prickle likes to explore and he loves apples," the mother hedgehog explained. "But he should have been home by now."

"Oh dear." Dazzle couldn't help feeling worried. She perched on a yellow daisy next to the hedgehogs.

Then she glanced at Mallow, Twinkle and Skipper. "Why don't we fly around the orchard and look for Prickle?" she suggested. "We can cover much more ground than the hedgehogs can!"

"That's such a good idea," agreed Mallow, giving a twirl.

"Of course!" said Skipper.

"Lets get started." Twinkle added.

"What does Prickle look like?" asked Mallow. "We'll need to be able to recognize him when we see him."

"Well, he looks like us," the father hedgehog replied. "Lots of needles on his back, round black eyes – that kind of thing. He's just smaller."

"We'll do our best to find him," said Skipper.

"Oh, thank you, butterflies," the father hedgehog said.

"We're kind as well as beautiful, you know," said Twinkle happily, bobbing in the air.

Dazzle tried not to smile. Twinkle was a Peacock butterfly and she was very proud of the beautiful colours and patterns on her wings.

"We'll head home and look after our other children," the mother hedgehog said, looking relieved. "You will let us know right away if you find Prickle, won't you?"

"Yes, of course," Dazzle promised.

"Thank you!" the hedgehogs cried, and they scuttled through the grass, their prickly behinds swinging from side to side.

"Come on, then," called Twinkle, batting her red and blue wings. "Let's find Prickle!"

CHAPTER TWO

That's No Hedgehog!

Dazzle and the other butterflies zigzagged their way between the apple trees. They flew close to the ground so that they wouldn't miss Prickle. They spotted squirrels scampering up and down tree trunks, bees busy collecting nectar and spiders spinning webs between the flower stalks.

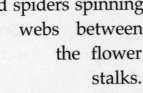

But there was no sign of a hedgehog anywhere.

Suddenly Twinkle gave a shout. "Oh! I can see something moving around in one of those bushes!"

She swooped down towards the bush. Mallow had flown on ahead, but Dazzle and Skipper followed Twinkle. Dazzle really hoped that they had found Prickle! The little hedgehog would probably be feeling lonely by now. Dazzle remembered how lost she'd felt on her first day out of her cocoon, before she'd found Butterfly Meadow and made friends.

"Hello?" Twinkle called, hovering in front of the bush. "Is that Prickle in there? Come out, whoever you are, please!"

There was a rustling of leaves. Dazzle held her breath, hoping to see the prickly spines of a hedgehog. But instead a furry brown creature with floppy ears popped its head out. It was a rabbit!

"Oh!" said Skipper. "Sorry to bother you. We thought you might be the hedgehog we're looking for."

The rabbit twitched it's nose. "Sorry, no hedgehog in here," he replied, hopping back into the bush.

Just then, the three butterflies heard Mallow calling them from up ahead. "Dazzle! Twinkle! Skipper! Over here!"

"It sounds like Mallow's found something," Dazzle said and darted away as fast as she could, with Skipper and Twinkle right behind her.

CHAPTER THREE

Follow the Apples!

Mallow was floating in the air nearby, waiting for her friends.

"Look!" she said, tipping her wing towards the ground.

Dazzle, Skipper and Twinkle glanced down and saw an apple core lying on the grass.

"Someone's been eating apples," Mallow went on. "Maybe it was Prickle."

"There's another half-eaten apple over there," said Dazzle, spotting one a little way off.

The group of butterflies fluttered over to the apple core and looked around.

"And there's another one!" Twinkle cried. "It's a trail of half-eaten apples!"

"Let's follow it," Skipper suggested. "It could lead us to Prickle."

The butterflies flew over the trail of apple cores, winding their way in and out of the trees.

"There are lots of apples, aren't there?" Mallow remarked. "And they all look as though someone's been munching on them."

"I'd have a stomach ache if I ate that many," Skipper added. Then she suddenly paused in mid-air. "I can hear something."

The other butterflies stopped.

"I hear something too," Dazzle whispered.

Mallow flew closer to the sound. "Look. Over here!"

Dazzle and the others swooped down to find a strange creature, sat on the grass munching on an apple. It was eating with loud slurps and Dazzle realized that was the noise she had heard. The creature had a long snout and spines just like a hedgehog, but it also had bits of apple stuck all over its face and a big  bump growing out of its back.

"What is it?" Dazzle asked her friends.

"Let's look closer," Twinkle suggested, quietly.

The butterflies dipped towards the ground. As they did, the strange creature suddenly glanced up and spotted them.

"What are you staring at?" the creature

asked in a squeaky voice. His mouth was full of apple and little pieces flew everywhere. Dazzle and the others had to dodge out of the way to avoid being hit by one of them!

Dazzle didn't mean to be rude and stare, but she'd *never* seen anything like this animal before in her life. This couldn't be Prickle, could it?

CHAPTER FOUR

Prickle in a Pickle

"We're sorry for staring," Skipper said politely, hovering in the air. "But we were wondering what kind of an animal you are?"

The creature glared at her.

"Well, I'm a hedgehog, of course!" he said. "Haven't you ever seen a hedgehog before?"

"I've never seen a hedgehog with a big bump on its back like you have," Dazzle told him.

"What are you talking about?" the hedgehog spluttered, looking embarrassed.

"I don't have a bump on my back!"

"Well, we're not making it up," Mallow said gently to the hedgehog. "Why don't you take a look for yourself?"

The hedgehog sighed loudly. He dropped the apple core he was munching and twisted round to look at his back. Then he twisted the other way. Soon he was going round and round in circles, trying to see. Dazzle and the other butterflies tried not to laugh.

"Well!" The hedgehog's spines were bristling with annoyance. "I think all you butterflies must have had a knock on the head – you're *seeing* things. There's nothing wrong with me!"

"How can he *not* know he has something sticking out of his back?" Twinkle whispered. Dazzle thought the same. She couldn't understand why the hedgehog kept insisting that nothing was wrong.

While the butterflies bobbed up and down in the air, Twinkle frowned. She lifted her face up and sniffed.

"Do you smell that?" she asked.

Twinkle allowed the breeze to blow her from one spot to another as she followed the smell. Then she flew closer to the ground until she was right above the hedgehog's bump.

Dazzle followed Twinkle. She noticed the smell, too! It was sweet and sharp all at the same time. Dazzle and Twinkle peered at the large, mushy bump on the hedgehog's back.

"Oh, now I see what it is," Twinkle cried. "It's a rotten apple. It must be stuck on his spines!"

The hedgehog looked embarrassed. "Er – well – yes," he said in his squeaky voice. "I thought I could feel something on my back. I knew it was there all along."

"You knew?" Mallow stared at him in surprise. "Then why did you pretend that there was nothing on your back?"

"I was just testing you," the hedgehog mumbled, shuffling his feet.

Dazzle didn't believe him. She huddled close to her butterfly friends. "I don't think he wants to admit that he needs our help," she murmured to the others.

"I wonder how the apple got stuck on his back in the first place?" Skipper said, forgetting to keep her voice down.

"Well, if you must know," the hedgehog said, "I was taking a nap. Eating apples can be hard work. I woke up when I felt a thump. But I didn't know what it was. I thought I'd dreamt it."

"It must have been the apple falling from the tree and landing on top of you," said Mallow. She flew around the hedgehog, inspecting him, carefully. "At least you're not hurt."

"Don't worry," Dazzle said kindly. "We'll help you get the apple off. We can't get too close to your prickly spines, as they might tear our wings. But I'm sure we'll think of something."

"No," the hedgehog replied quickly, "I don't need any help! I'm perfectly all right, thank you. I'm just going to finish my nap, now. Goodbye."

He squeezed his eyes tight shut.

"He's only pretending to go to sleep, I'm sure of it," Mallow said in a low voice as the hedgehog began to snore loudly. "He can't be comfortable with an apple stuck there like that!"

"He won't be able to walk properly either," Skipper pointed out. "That apple looks heavy."

"What should we do now?" asked Twinkle. "We can't just leave him like this!"

CHAPTER FIVE

Upside Down

Dazzle watched as Skipper flew over to the hedgehog and landed on his nose.

"Do you mind?" the hedgehog grumbled, opening his eyes. His spines bristled, standing up fiercely.

"You could be a little nicer to us," Skipper pointed out, still balancing on the hedgehog's nose. "We are only trying to help."

"Why do you want to help me?" the hedgehog asked.

"We've spent all this time looking for

you," Mallow said, swirling and twirling in the air above. "We're not going to abandon you now."

"Looking for me? Why?" the hedgehog asked. He looked at Dazzle and each of her friends in turn.

"Is your name Prickle?" asked Skipper.

"How do you know that?" the hedgehog asked. As he spoke, he reached out for one of the apples near to him on the ground. Dazzle had to swoop between him and the apple to stop him trying to take a bite. *No more apples for you!* she thought, grinning.

"Your mum and dad are worried about you," Skipper explained. She hovered in front of an apple on the other side of Prickle to stop him from trying to eat that one, too.

"And we said we'd help them to find you," Dazzle added.

"You really should go home right away," Mallow chimed in.

Prickle gave up trying to reach the apples. He stared at his feet. "I *do* want to go home," he admitted at last. His tummy gave a loud growl. "I'm not even supposed to be in the orchard this late. But I can't get home with this apple on my back. It's too difficult to walk. Please, will you help me?"

"Of course we'll help you, Prickle," Dazzle piped up, flying a loop in the air in her excitement. "We just have to work out how." She glanced at the other butterflies. "Any ideas?"

"Look how rough the bark of this apple tree is," Twinkle said suddenly. "Maybe Prickle could use the tree trunk to scratch the apple off his spines?"

"Oh, that's a great idea, Twinkle," Dazzle agreed. "Prickle, do you think you can walk over to the tree?"

Prickle sighed as his tummy growled again. "I'll try," he replied.

The butterflies flew around Prickle as he took one step forward, then another. Dazzle could see that the apple on the hedgehog's

back was very heavy. It made him sway from side to side.

"Ooh, my tummy hurts!" Prickle groaned, as he took another unsteady step.

"I think I've eaten too many apples!"

"Not far now, Prickle," Skipper said. She flew backwards leading Prickle along. "Come on, just another couple of steps towards me."

But suddenly Prickle tripped over a piece of apple lying in the grass and lost his balance. Dazzle gasped as the hedgehog

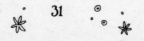

31

toppled over on to his side. Panting, Prickle tried desperately to roll himself back up. He almost managed to get himself the right way up, but then he stumbled. This time he landed on his back, his four little paws waving helplessly in the air.

"Oh no!" Twinkle cried, zooming down towards him. "Can you try to turn over again, Prickle?"

"No!" the hedgehog gasped. "I can't move."

"And look, the apple's really stuck on his spines now," Dazzle pointed out. "This is a disaster!"

Dazzle felt terrible. She and her friends had only been trying to help, and now they'd made things worse.

"Let's see if we can push Prickle back over," she suggested to the others.

The four butterflies took hold of Prickle's

little paws and tried to rock him upright. Dazzle leaned against one of Prickle's feet

and tried to push, but her wings got in the way. She could see that Prickle was hardly moving at all. The hedgehog was just too big for them.

"Ooh!" Prickle groaned, stranded on his back. "I feel *really* ill now. My tummy hurts and I feel sick!"

"We need to get him on his feet, and fast!" Mallow cried.

CHAPTER SIX

Let's Tickle Prickle

"I've had an idea! I think I know how we can help Prickle get back on his feet," Dazzle said.

"How?" Skipper asked. "He's much too heavy for us to lift!"

"And we can't get too close to his prickly spines," Twinkle added, looking nervous.

"Listen!' said Dazzle, lowering her voice so that Prickle couldn't hear. "If we all take turns tickling Prickle with our wings, maybe he'll laugh so much that he'll rock back on to his feet!"

Dazzle's friends smiled cheekily.

"Sounds like fun," Skipper said.

Mallow and Twinkle flew over to Prickle. Mallow landed on one of Prickle's front paws and Twinkle fluttered down on to the other. Then, as Dazzle and Skipper watched,

the two butterflies began to lightly tickle the hedgehog's paws with their wings.

"What are you doing?" Prickle yelped. "Ha, ha, ha! Stop! It tickles! Hee, hee, hee!"

Skipper and Dazzle flew over to Prickle and landed lightly on his nose.

"Your tiny butterfly feet are tickling me!" Prickle chortled, making Dazzle and Skipper laugh too.

Prickle began to squirm around, moving this way and that. Dazzle watched hopefully as he rocked backwards and forwards, rolling about with laughter. Would the hedgehog be able to get on his feet?

"Oh, I'm going to sneeze!" Prickle said suddenly.

Quickly, the butterflies flew out of the way.

"*A-a-a-a-tishoo!*" Prickle gave a huge sneeze. He rocked forwards sharply and Dazzle's wings trembled with excitement.

But even though Prickle's paws grazed the grass, the force of the sneeze wasn't quite enough to get him the right way up. He rolled on to his back again and stared unhappily at the butterflies in the sky above him.

"That nearly worked! But please don't do it again," Prickle said. "I don't think I can take much more tickling!"

"So what should we do *now*?" Mallow asked her friends.

Dazzle thought hard. She was determined not to leave Prickle stuck in the orchard. There simply *had* to be a way to get the hedgehog back on his feet.

"Do you remember when we were bouncing on the see-saw leaf this morning?" Dazzle said. "Maybe we can make a see-saw for Prickle?"

"That's brilliant, Dazzle!" said Mallow.

"You mean we're going to send Prickle shooting through the air?" Twinkle asked. "I've never seen a flying hedgehog before!"

"Hedgehogs can't fly!" Prickle called, looking worried. "We like to be on the ground!"

"It's a great idea, Dazzle," said Skipper. "But how are we going to make it work? We're not strong enough to bounce Prickle up into the air ourselves, and what if he hurts himself when he lands?"

"Yes, we need a safety net to catch Prickle," Dazzle replied. She pointed with her wing at two spiders who were spinning large, glittering webs in a nearby bush. "I thought we could ask the spiders to weave us a web between those two apple trees."

"Good thinking, Dazzle!" Twinkle said, nodding her head.

"And remember the squirrels we saw earlier?" Dazzle went on. "They could help us make a see-saw from a tree branch. The squirrels are much bigger than we are, so *they* could be the ones who jump on to the other side of the see-saw and send Prickle flying."

Prickle had been listening to all this, and he looked *very* nervous.

"Do you really think this is going to work?" he called. Dazzle could understand

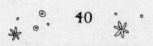

why he was worried, but she and her friends had to do whatever it took to help Prickle back to his mum and dad.

"We have to *try*," Dazzle said. "It's our only chance."

CHAPTER SEVEN

Can Hedgehogs Fly?

"Twinkle, you and Mallow go and round up some spiders," Dazzle instructed. "Skipper and I will find the squirrels." Listening to herself, Dazzle realized how much more confident she was now, than when she'd first emerged from her cocoon as a shy young butterfly. *I just hope my plan works*, she thought.

Twinkle and Mallow darted off while Dazzle and Skipper flew up among the trees.

"Don't worry, Prickle," Skipper called back. "We'll have you on your feet in no time."

Dazzle and Skipper wove between the branches. After a moment, they spotted two squirrels near the top of a tree. The squirrels were chattering excitedly as they hid a pile of nuts in a hole inside part of the trunk.

"Hello," Dazzle called.

"Ooh, butterflies!" the smaller of the two squirrels exclaimed. "Aren't you pretty?"

"Thank you," Dazzle replied. "We were wondering if you could give us a helping hand?" Dazzle explained what had happened to Prickle and told the squirrel about her see-saw idea.

"Oh, the poor hedgehog!" the smaller squirrel

exclaimed. "Of course we'll help! Let's go right away!"

The two squirrels scampered down the tree trunk, their bushy tails waving, and Dazzle and Skipper flew after them. The squirrels soon arrived at the bottom of the tree, and hopped excitedly around a fallen branch.

"Look, we've found the perfect see-saw!" one of the squirrels called to Dazzle and Skipper.

"That's wonderful," Dazzle said gratefully.

"Here come Mallow and Twinkle." Skipper pointed a wing at their friends, who were flying back through the trees towards them. "And look, Dazzle! They've gathered a whole army of spiders!"

Dazzle saw a long line of spiders walking through the grass on their spindly legs.

45

"Thanks, Mallow and Twinkle!" she called. "And thank you, spiders, for coming to help."

The spiders all stopped, and the one at the front of the line stared at poor Prickle.

"Hmm," he said, "We're going to need an extra-strong net." He turned to the other spiders. "OK, let's get spinning, guys!"

The spiders began to spin a sturdy net between two of the trees. Meanwhile the squirrels dragged the fallen branch over to Prickle.

"One end of the branch has to go underneath him," Dazzle directed. "Prickle, could you rock yourself just a little so that the squirrels can slide the branch under your back?"

"I hope this works," Prickle sighed as he rolled to one side. "Otherwise I'm going to be here for ever!"

"Try to think positive, Prickle!" Mallow called.

But Dazzle had noticed that Prickle's spines were trembling. She flew over to him.

"Are you all right, Prickle?" she asked
softly.

"I'm *afraid* to fly," he admitted.

"Flying's so much fun," Dazzle assured
him.

"Yes – if you have wings!" Prickle
muttered, looking unhappy.

"Look, the spiders have spun a really
strong net to catch you." Dazzle pointed her
wing at the enormous, glistening cobweb.
"All you have to do is trust us. We're your
friends."

The two squirrels scampered back up the

tree and positioned themselves over one end of the see-saw. Then the spiders crawled to the edges of the net, safely out of harm's way.

Mallow, Twinkle and Skipper hovered nearby, watching anxiously.

"Ready?" Dazzle asked the hedgehog. "Can you trust us?"

Prickle hesitated, then gave a firm nod of his head. Dazzle felt herself flush with happiness – he was going to do it!

"Close your eyes and get ready, Prickle!" Dazzle said.

"I'm ready," Prickle whispered, his voice shaking.

Dazzle looked up at the squirrels. "One, two, three! GO!" she cried.

The two squirrels launched themselves out of the tree and soared through the air.

"Wheee!" they both cried out. They landed with a thump on one end of the see-saw.

Prickle shot up into the air.

He was flying!

CHAPTER EIGHT

Back Home

Dazzle watched as Prickle zoomed through the air towards the spiders' net.

"Here I come!" Prickle shouted.

Everyone watched as the hedgehog landed in the cobweb net with a thump. He bounced a few times but the net didn't break.

"Let's hear it for Prickle!" the biggest spider yelled. "Hip, hip – hooray!"

Everyone cheered.

"Prickle, you did it!" Dazzle cried, zooming over to the net. "You're the bravest hedgehog *ever*!"

"I was very scared," Prickle admitted, "but it was fun!"

The spiders rushed forward to help him get down, and he rolled carefully out of the net. The apple that had been wedged on Prickle's spines was left behind, caught in the fine, sticky threads of the cobweb.

"I'm free!" Prickle cried happily as he reached the ground. He gave himself a shake. "Thank you, spiders. Thank you, squirrels. But most of all, thank you, butterflies!"

Dazzle, Twinkle, Mallow and Skipper swooped down and peppered Prickle's cheeks with soft butterfly kisses. Prickle blushed, but he also looked pleased.

"I won't forget all my new butterfly friends," he said. "I know I wasn't very nice before, but I will be a better friend from now on."

"We won't forget you, either, Prickle," Dazzle replied. "After all, who could forget a flying hedgehog?"

They all laughed at that, even Prickle.

"It's time for us all to go home," said Skipper. She turned to Prickle. "Your parents will still be wondering where you are." Prickle's tummy gave a loud growl.

"I hope they won't expect me to have any supper," he said. Dazzle felt laughter fizzing up inside her.

"You might not need to eat anything for quite a while," she agreed. "Definitely no more apples!"

"Goodbye," the spiders called as the four friends and Prickle set off.

"See you later!" shouted the squirrels, scurrying back up the tree.

The butterflies went with Prickle back to the place where they'd met his mum and dad.

"I know my way from here," Prickle said. "Thank you again, for everything."

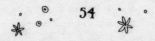

The sun was beginning to set and the sky was streaked with red. Up ahead, Dazzle could see the long grasses and dancing flowers of Butterfly Meadow. She didn't think she'd ever seen her home looking as beautiful as it did today.

"Goodbye!" the butterflies called out as Prickle strolled through the grass towards his home. His bottom swayed from side to side but now there was no big red apple attached to his spines.

"He looks just like a normal hedgehog again," Mallow commented, as the butterflies swooped through the air back to the meadow.

"Except he isn't a normal hedgehog. He's a flying hedgehog!" Dazzle said, laughing. She couldn't wait to tell all their other butterfly friends about Prickle. He'd been part of their best adventure yet.

Want to know all about the butterflies
in the meadow?

Dazzle

Pale Clouded Yellow butterfly

Likes: Dancing and making friends

Dislikes: Being left out

Twinkle

Peacock butterfly

Likes: Her beautiful wings

Dislikes: Getting wet!

Mallow

Cabbage White butterfly

Likes: Organizing parties and activities

Dislikes: Being bored

Skipper

Holly Blue butterfly

Likes: Helping others

Dislikes: Birds who try to eat her!

Read about more adventures in
Butterfly Meadow

FLUTTERY, FRIENDLY FUN

Butterfly Meadow

Dazzle's First Day

Olivia Moss

FLUTTERY, FRIENDLY FUN

Butterfly Meadow

Twinkle Dives In

Olivia Moss

FLUTTERY, FRIENDLY FUN

Butterfly Meadow

Mallow's Top Team

Olivia Moss

FLUTTERY, FRIENDLY FUN

Butterfly Meadow

Skipper to the Rescue

Olivia Moss

FLUTTERY, FRIENDLY FUN

Butterfly
Meadow

Twinkle and the
Busy Bee

Olivia Moss